FUN AND GAMES

The Wild World of Birding

Using Ratios

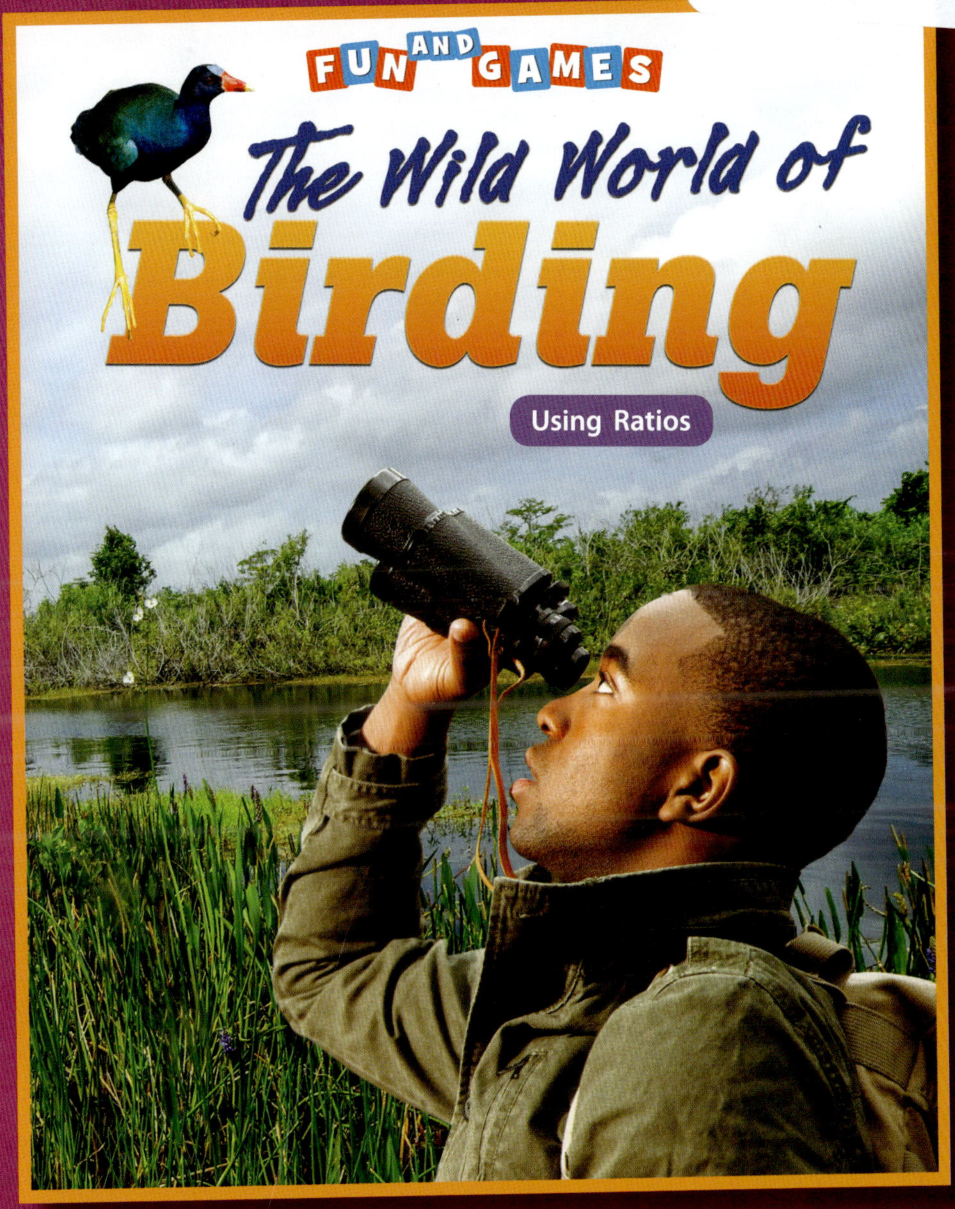

June Kikuchi

Contributing Author

Alison S. Marzocchi, Ph.D.

Consultant

Colleen Pollitt, M.A.Ed.
Math Support Teacher
Howard County Public Schools

Publishing Credits

Rachelle Cracchiolo, M.S.Ed., *Publisher*
Conni Medina, M.A.Ed., *Editor in Chief*
Dona Herweck Rice, *Series Developer*
Emily R. Smith, M.A.Ed., *Series Developer*
Diana Kenney, M.A.Ed., NBCT, *Content Director*
Stacy Monsman, M.A., *Editor*
Michelle Jovin, M.A., *Associate Editor*
Fabiola Sepulveda, *Graphic Designer*

Image Credits: p.8 (top) Howard Lipin/ZUMAPRESS/Newscom; p.12 Gerald Marella / Shutterstock; p.16 (bottom center) Andy Cripe / Associated Press; p.18 Marvin Pfeiffer/ ZUMA Press/Newscom; p.20–21 Jennifer Simonson/ZUMA Press/Newscom; p.22 (bottom) Shauna Stephenson / Associated Press; p.24 Courtesy of the Cornell Lab of Ornithology, Oxford University and Benjamin Van Doren and Kyle Horton; all other images Shutterstock and / or iStock

Library of Congress Cataloging-in-Publication Data

Names: Kikuchi, June, author.
Title: The wild world of birding : using ratios / June Kikuchi.
Description: Huntington Beach, CA : Teacher Created Materials, [2019] | Series: Fun and games | Audience: Grade 4 to 6. | Includes index. | Identifiers: LCCN 2018047786 (print) | LCCN 2018048457 (ebook) | ISBN 9781425855253 (eBook) | ISBN 9781425858810 (paperback)
Subjects: LCSH: Bird watching--Juvenile literature.
Classification: LCC QL677.5 (ebook) | LCC QL677.5 .K536 2019 (print) | DDC 598.072/34--dc23
LC record available at https://lccn.loc.gov/2018047786

Teacher Created Materials
5301 Oceanus Drive
Huntington Beach, CA 92649-1030
www.tcmpub.com

ISBN 978-1-4258-5881-0

Printed in Malaysia
Thumbprints.21254

Table of Contents

Bird as a Verb

What is birding? To *bird* simply means to watch birds in the wild, and the people who bird are called *birders*. Some people are casual birders. They put out hummingbird feeders in the summer to attract those buzzing aerial acrobats. Or they have seed feeders for finches, quail, and sparrows.

Other people are more serious about birding. They keep lists of the birds they have seen and continually add to them. They are the ones who notice when warblers return to North America in the spring. Many birders travel to see as many birds as they can.

A ruby-throated hummingbird drinks from a feeder.

How popular is birding? According to the U.S. Fish and Wildlife Survey, more than 86 million people in the United States watch wildlife. Of this number, over 45 million people watch only birds. That's almost equal to the number of people who live in Spain!

Birding is popular because it's easy to do and anyone can join in the fun! No special equipment is required, although most birders use binoculars and a field guide. In no time at all, beginners will want to do their part to help birds and protect their habitats. That's why birders are also called naturalists, environmentalists, and preservationists.

Do you have a sense of adventure and a love of the outdoors and nature? Then birding may be for you!

pileated woodpecker

LET'S EXPLORE MATH

About 45,000,000 of the 86,000,000 people who watch wildlife only watch birds.

1. What is the simplified ratio of people who only watch birds to people who watch wildlife?
2. How can you tell whether the percent of wildlife watchers who only watch birds is greater or less than 50%?

Some Twists and Lists

People can watch birds anywhere—in cities, in the country, by the water, and in the mountains. Birding is a year-round hobby. There are more birds to see in the spring and summer, when many birds return to the United States to **breed**. But fall and winter are exciting times to bird too. During the fall, birders can see large numbers of migrating birds, including large hawks that soar in the air. And there are plenty of hearty **species** that stay throughout cold winters.

Black-capped chickadees stay throughout the winter.

Once people start to notice birds, they likely will want to identify which species they are seeing. That's when things get more challenging and more fun. The Cornell Lab of **Ornithology** is part of Cornell University in New York, and its goal is to study birds. According to the lab, there are six key characteristics to identifying birds—size, shape, color pattern, behavior, **field marks**, and habitat. If people take note of these six things, they will have a good chance of identifying the bird in front of them.

Sounds easy, right? Wrong! Male and female birds often look different from each other. Males are usually more colorful than females. To complicate things further, some males have bright, colorful **plumage** during the breeding season and duller, drabber feathering during the rest of the year.

Northern cardinal females have brown plumage, while males have red plumage.

Cattle egrets have golden feathers on their heads during breeding season, but they are entirely white when not breeding.

To help identify birds, most birders use a field guide, which can be a book, website, or app. A field guide lists a bird's information accompanied by a photo or illustration to compare colors and markings. A range map shows where the bird is found. And a short description of the bird's behavior and call can help in identification. Apps and websites sometimes include a sound clip of a bird's call, so birders can identify it by ear.

LET'S EXPLORE MATH

Garrett's hummingbird feeder holds 40 ounces of sugar water. The sugar water recipe calls for 8 ounces of sugar and 32 ounces of water.

Part	Whole
	10
8	40
	100

1. What percent of the sugar water is sugar? Use the rate table to solve.
2. Write the percent of sugar in the sugar water as a fraction and decimal.
3. What percent of the sugar water is water? Explain your reasoning.
4. Write the percent of water in the sugar water as a fraction and a decimal.

Start at Home

So, how and where do birders get started? Many people begin at home and identify the birds they see in their backyards or in their neighborhoods.

Birders often **lure** birds to their yards (or porches or balconies) by planting flowers that birds feed on. Hummingbirds like nectar-producing plants, such as bee balm and honeysuckle. Seed-eating cardinals, chickadees, and goldfinches like coneflowers or black-eyed Susans. Many birds also eat berries.

Birders who don't have **green thumbs** can still offer food to birds. They can put out a seed feeder or a hummingbird feeder filled with sugar water. Like all animals, birds need water. Whether it is a simple pan of water or an elaborate birdbath, both will provide birds with water for drinking and bathing.

Once you're all set up, it's time to identify birds! Is that raspberry-colored bird a house finch or a purple finch?

purple finch

house finch

Keep a List or Two

Once people get the hang of identifying birds, they may want to keep a tally of all the species they have seen. Many start with a home or backyard list. Even presidents have kept home lists! Theodore Roosevelt reportedly birded on the grounds of the White House and around Washington, DC. He later wrote a list of over 90 birds he saw during his presidency.

After birders have healthy backyard lists, they might want to **compile** other lists. Does a birder live near a national park or a well-known birding area? If they visit regularly, they might consider having a list dedicated to that location.

Once a birder has been bitten by the birding bug, they may want to look for birds everywhere. Some people have lists of the birds they have seen on their commute to and from work or school. Many birders keep vacation lists. The list of possible birding lists is endless!

Instead of maintaining several lists, many birders opt to have just one list, which is called a *life list*. This is a record of all the bird species they have seen in their lives.

A birder adds a new species to her life list.

LET'S EXPLORE MATH

On Shari's class field trip to Washington, DC, she spotted some of the same species of birds that past presidents have spotted. She tracked her sightings in a table. Help analyze her data.

1. Shari notices that one species represents 50% of the birds she spotted. How can you tell which species this is?
2. What percent of the birds Shari spotted are downy woodpeckers? Use the percent bars to solve.
3. How can you tell whether red-tailed hawks represent more or less than 10% of the birds Shari spotted?

Bird	Number Spotted
Carolina chickadee	15
northern cardinal	4
downy woodpecker	9
red-tailed hawk	2
TOTAL	30

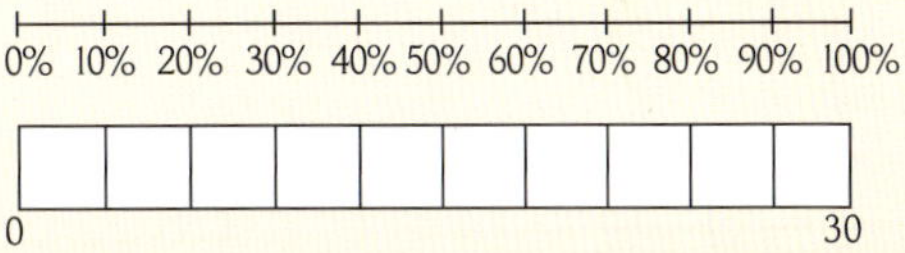

Go Big!

Things get a little outrageous when it comes to competitive events, such as Big Days and Big Years. Whether it is for a day or an entire year, birders go to great lengths to record the most birds they can.

Big Days

As its name implies, a Big Day lasts for 24 hours, during which birders look for as many birds as they can in a given area. One of the most popular Big Day events is the annual World Series of Birding (WSB) sponsored by the New Jersey Audubon Society and the Cape May Bird **Observatory** (CMBO). For over 35 years, teams of birders **converge** in New Jersey for one long day in May to look for birds.

From midnight to midnight, teams **disperse** to search for birds all over the Garden State, which is New Jersey's nickname. Some teams travel around the entire state. Other teams concentrate on a limited area within the state. There are youth teams and senior teams, so people of all ages have fun!

Pete Dunne, the former director of the CMBO, started the WSB in 1984. The event has been called a marathon and a challenge. "This is birding. We're turbocharged," Dunne said about the WSB in a 2013 interview.

The Cape May Hawk Watch was CMBO's first organized bird-counting event.

indigo bunting

Cape May warbler

American oystercatcher

Photographers snap photos of rare terns at Cape May.

Like most Big Days, the WSB has rules that all teams must follow. For example, 95 percent of the birds on a team's list must be seen or heard by every member of the team. Another rule specifies that eggs do not count as birds. Although trophies are awarded, the goal of the event is to raise awareness and money for bird conservation in New Jersey through sponsors and pledges.

Awareness is something that all birders support and promote. In fact, Dunne regularly encourages birders who can't make it to New Jersey for the WSB to "join in by doing your own local Big Day. Walk around your yard or neighborhood," he said. "Stop. Listen. Look. How many birds can you identify?"

Big Sits

A more relaxing version of the Big Day is the Big Sit, where birders record the birds they see from one relatively large spot. A birder picks a place to "sit" and then marks off a 17-foot (5-meter) **diameter** circle around it. For the next 24 hours, they will count the number of birds seen or heard while staying within the circle. *Bird Watcher's Digest* magazine sponsors an annual Big Sit in October, and birders from around the world participate.

LET'S EXPLORE MATH

According to the WSB's rules, 95% of the birds on a team's list must be seen or heard by every member of the team. Imagine that a team spots 200 birds. How many birds must be spotted by every member? Represent the birds on a hundreds grid like this one. Use it to solve the problem.

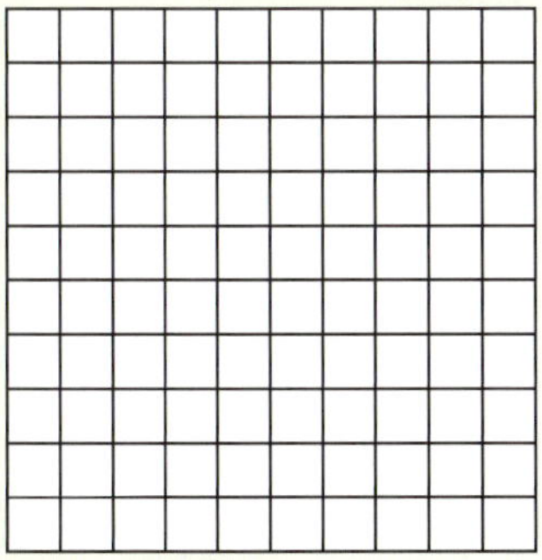

☐ = _____ birds

Big Years

Big Years are for hard-core birders who spend an entire year traveling around the world to find birds. Not many people can take off for a whole year, but in 2015, an American birder named Noah Strycker did just that. "I set out to see the world, one bird at a time," he said. He traveled over 100,000 miles (160,934 kilometers), seeing 41 countries and all 7 continents. Strycker wanted to see half of the more than 10,000 bird species in the world. He surpassed this goal. He saw 6,042 birds in 365 days. He smashed the former Big Year record of 4,341 birds.

Strycker wrote a daily blog for the National Audubon Society's website (www.audubon.org) during his amazing year. He also wrote a book about his yearlong adventure. Both the blog and the book are titled *Birding Without Borders*.

Strycker in his backyard

Strycker spotted some rare species during his Big Year, including a spoon-billed sandpiper (top) and a harpy eagle (bottom).

People thought Strycker's record would stand for years. But a year later, a Danish birder named Arjan Dwarshuis (AHR-ee-ehn DVAHRS-hoys) beat it. He tallied 6,852 bird species in 2016.

Time will tell if this record will be broken. But wherever birders go, they should take Strycker's advice. He said, "When traveling the world, it pays to tip well, smile always, arrive early, be nice, and carry a spoon in your back pocket (in case a jar of peanut butter turns up)!"

Dwarshuis holds up a sign in Costa Rica after he spotted his 6,119th bird.

LET'S EXPLORE MATH

There are about 10,000 recognized bird species in the world. In 2016, Arjan Dwarshuis spotted almost 7,000 of them. Imagine that he wants to estimate his sightings.

1. Use the approximate numbers to write the bird species he spotted as a fraction out of 100.
2. What approximate percent of recognized bird species did he spot?
3. How can you tell whether the actual percent of recognized bird species he spotted is greater or less than the approximate percent?

Birding Ethics and Rules

Most birders and birding events adhere to the Code of Birding Ethics. These rules about birding manners were developed by the American Birding Association (ABA). The organization is a leader among birders and birding groups in North America. Its mission is "to inspire all people to enjoy and protect wild birds."

The ABA Code of Birding Ethics ensures the safety of wild birds. The code has four main rules:

1. Promote the welfare of birds and their environment.
2. Respect the law and the rights of others.
3. Ensure that feeders, nest structures, and other artificial bird environments are safe.
4. Group birding, whether organized or **impromptu**, requires special care.

A group of birders looks for wild birds without disturbing their environments.

These guidelines make a lot of sense. And they are easy to follow.

The ABA sponsors Big Days throughout the year. Birders must follow the Big Day rules to record their counts on ABA's website. The ABA also has rules for Big Year participants.

To add a bird to a life list or to an official list during a Big Day, birders should follow the ABA's recording rules. Again, maintaining the welfare of the birds is always the most important rule. One of the recording rules states that "the bird must have been alive, wild, and unrestrained when encountered." Another rule says that "the bird must have been encountered under conditions that conform to the ABA Code of Birding Ethics."

Citizen Science

Scientists often rely on birders to collect data. Birders volunteer to count the birds they see. They also maintain **nest box** trails to help bluebirds or kestrels. These programs are called *citizen science*. For birders, it's fun to be part of scientific research by doing something they enjoy.

The longest-running citizen science program for birds is the Christmas Bird Count. It is sponsored by the National Audubon Society. The first Christmas Bird Count was in 1900—more than 100 years ago! It started as a Christmas Day event but has since changed. Today, volunteer birders spend one winter day in December or January counting birds. They must stay within a 15 mi. (24 km) **radius**. Each count circle has 10 or more volunteers, including a compiler who manages the group.

Birders in Minnesota participate in the Christmas Bird Count.

Counting Backyard Birds

Many citizen science projects rely on the huge number of backyard birders. These are people who primarily enjoy watching birds at home.

The Great Backyard Bird Count takes place over four days in February. Birders are asked to spend 15 minutes or longer counting the birds they see in their backyards.

A birder tries to attract birds by filling his backyard feeder.

LET'S EXPLORE MATH

Imagine that a count circle spots 400 warblers during the Christmas Bird Count. The compiler reports that 83% of the birds were yellow-rumped warblers. The remaining warblers were different species.

1. Which expression can you use to calculate the number of yellow-rumped warblers?

   A. $400 \times \frac{83}{100}$ **C.** $400 \div 83$

   B. 400×83 **D.** $400 \div \frac{83}{100}$

2. Use the correct expression to find the number of yellow-rumped warblers the count circle spots.

3. What percent of warblers spotted by the count circle were different species of warblers? How many birds is this?

Project FeederWatch is another program that is interested in backyard birds. Volunteers watch the birds that visit their feeders during the winter. This project started in Canada in the 1970s.

Scientists look at the data collected during the Christmas Bird Count, the Great Backyard Bird Count, and Project FeederWatch. They learn about the **fluctuations** in winter bird populations.

Nesting Birds

American kestrel

Many birds use nest boxes, or birdhouses, to lay their eggs. A popular species that uses nest boxes is the bluebird. Bluebirders put up nest boxes in their backyards or neighborhoods. Then, they monitor their trail of boxes. They count how many nest boxes are used. They also count how many eggs are laid and how many hatch. Most importantly, they report how many baby bluebirds **fledge** and fly away. Many states have bluebird societies that give advice on starting bluebird trails.

HawkWatch International in Utah runs a similar program that focuses on the American kestrel. The kestrel is the smallest **falcon** in North America. Its population has been in decline for years.

Birders can help nesting birds through other citizen science programs. The Smithsonian leads Neighborhood Nestwatch in Washington, DC. The Cornell Lab runs NestWatch. This program has people become certified nestwatchers.

A birder searches for falcons on behalf of HawkWatch International.

An Eastern bluebird brings food to a nest box.

Eastern bluebird carrying a worm

Eastern bluebird hatchlings and eggs

BirdCast

The Cornell Lab also runs BirdCast. Data for BirdCast is collected from birders around the United States, as well as from weather radar stations. The radar data comes from 143 stations positioned around the United States. They update every 10 minutes and can even tell which directions birds are flying!

BirdCast uses computers to predict where and when birds will migrate. However, radar cannot currently tell specific species, so BirdCast still relies on birders for species identification.

Currently, BirdCast can only predict migration patterns in the United States. Their predictions are based on radar data, and not all countries' radar systems work with those in the United States. However, BirdCast's workers hope to make it a global project one day!

The kind of information birders can learn from websites like BirdCast is amazing. And as these websites become more accurate and easier to use, the future of birding is soaring high!

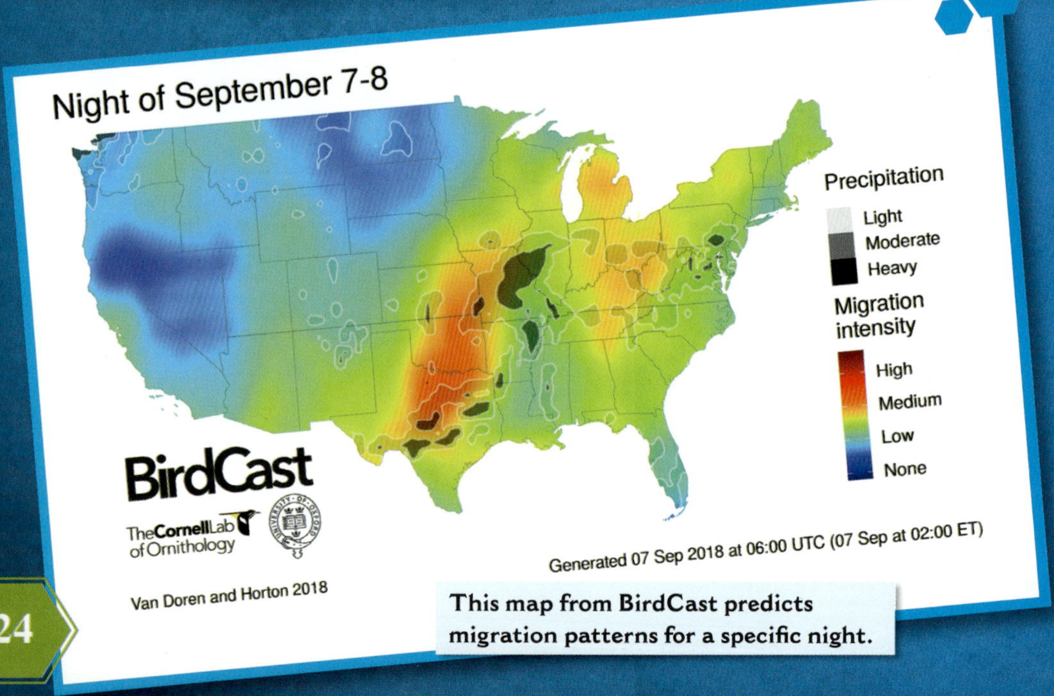

This map from BirdCast predicts migration patterns for a specific night.

LET'S EXPLORE MATH

BirdCast's most popular feature is its tracking of the flight paths of migrating birds. Biologists use another technique for tracking migrating birds—*banding*. Every year, biologists carefully catch migratory birds, band their feet, and release them. Biologists hope to catch and release the banded birds again at different locations to track migration.

Imagine that three biologists report their data:

- Dr. Jenkins recaptured 28 of the 560 birds she banded.
- Dr. Alvi banded 850 birds but did not recapture 799 of them.
- Dr. Rao recaptured 34 of her banded birds but did not recapture 391 of them.

1. Which biologist recaptured the greatest number of banded birds?
2. Which biologist recaptured the greatest percent of banded birds?
3. Is the same biologist the answer for questions 1 and 2? Why or why not?

A biologist bands an osprey.

Get Started

So much of our lives are spent rushing from one place to another. We are **bombarded** by calls, texts, emails, chores, school or work, friends, and family. It's overwhelming.

Why not escape from it all? Simply follow the instructions of Pete Dunne, the founder of the WSB in New Jersey. Go outside, stop, listen, and look.

birders in the Amazon

That's all you need to do to start birding. Once you take that first step, you'll see aspects of nature you never could have imagined. Every outing is an adventure that could bring with it new birds and new friends. Birders are kind and usually eager and happy to help fellow birders, especially beginners. If you come upon a group of birders peering into a tree, ask them what species they're looking at. They will help you identify all those little birds darting through the branches. They'll teach you how to filter one bird's song out of what may sound like a **cacophony** of chirping and noise, or they can give you tips to determine what that faraway hawk soaring in the sky might be.

Besides being a great social activity, birding is healthy, relaxing, and fun! Sign up for a birding trip with a local birding club, put up a feeder in your backyard, or volunteer for the next Christmas Bird Count. Just grab your binoculars and go. You won't regret it!

A group of chestnut-headed bee eaters perches on a branch.

Problem Solving

Hawk Mountain in Kempton, Pennsylvania, is a famed location for spotting raptors, or birds of prey, during fall and spring migration seasons. Imagine that you are a conservation scientist at Hawk Mountain. During a migration season, birders report their sightings to you. Use the data on page 29 to compile a report for the season, and design a brochure to attract more birders to Hawk Mountain.

1. Find the total season count of raptors. Use it to calculate the percent of the total season count each raptor group represents.

2. Your supervisor has some additional information but has questions about it. Use your data to answer them.

   a. Of the vultures spotted, 95% of them were turkey vultures. How many turkey vultures were spotted?

   b. There were 160 red-shouldered hawks spotted this season. This is 2% of all the female hawks spotted. How many female hawks were spotted?

3. Design an informational brochure that will attract birders to Hawk Mountain. Remember to include attention-getting graphics. Include at least three percents, fractions, or decimals. Write a brief summary for your supervisor, explaining the meaning of each number.

Raptor Group	Season Count	Percent of Total Season Count
vultures	680	
eagles	510	
hawks	14,790	
falcons	170	
other	850	
total		

Glossary

bombarded—constantly subjected to something

breed—to produce offspring

cacophony—loud, harsh sounds

compile—to create a list of something

converge—come together in one place

diameter—distance across a circle passing through a center point

disperse—to travel in different directions

falcon—a type of hawk

field marks—markings and patterns that distinguish species of birds from each other

fledge—mature to the point of having feathers to be able to leave the nest

fluctuations—changes in the numbers, levels, strengths, or values of things

green thumbs—the ability to make plants grow

impromptu—not prepared ahead of time

lure—to attract someone or something to go somewhere or do something

nest box—a box someone builds for birds to nest and breed in

observatory—a building where people conduct research and other activities about a certain topic

ornithology—the study of birds

plumage—the feathers of a bird

radius—a line from the center point to the outer edge of a circle or sphere

species—a group of animals or plants that share similar traits and can reproduce

Index

Answer Key

Let's Explore Math

page 5

1. 45:86
2. greater than 50%; Explanations will vary but may include 50% is half. Half of 86 is 43, so 45 is greater.

page 8

1. 20%; 2; 20
2. $\frac{20}{100}$, or $\frac{1}{5}$; 0.2, or 0.20
3. 80%; The sugar water is 20% sugar, and the rest is water. 100% – 20% = 80%
4. $\frac{80}{100}$, or $\frac{4}{5}$; 0.8, or 0.80

page 11

1. Carolina chickadee; Half, or 50%, of 30 is 15.
2. 30%
3. less; 10% of 30 is 3, and Shari spotted 2 red-tailed hawks.

page 15

each ☐ represents 2 birds; 190 birds

page 17

1. $\frac{70}{100}$
2. 70%
3. less; The actual number of sightings is less than 7,000, and the actual number of recognized bird species is greater than 10,000. So, the actual percent is less than the estimate.

page 21

1. A
2. 332 yellow-rumped warblers
3. 17%; 68 birds

page 25

1. Dr. Alvi (51 birds)
2. Dr. Rao (8%)
3. no; Dr. Alvi and Dr. Rao banded different total numbers of birds.

Problem Solving

1. **total:** 17,000, 100%;
   vultures: 4%; eagles; 3%;
   hawks: 87%; falcons: 1%;
   other: 5%
2. **a.** 646 turkey vultures

   b. 8,000 female hawks
3. Brochures should include graphics and at least three percents, fractions, or decimals. Summaries should include explanations of numbers included on the brochures.